JAGANNATHA OF P

* ANCIENT ORISSA

HIS QUESTION WAS ANSWERED THAT NIGHT IN A DREAM.
O KING, BEHOLD THIS HILL! IT IS NAMED NILACHALA. ON THIS HILL IS A CAVE.
INSIDE THE CAVE YOU WILL FIND THE MOST BEAUTIFUL IMAGE EVER SEEN OF NILAMADHAV — THE BLUE-COLOURED KRISHNA.
I'VE FOUND HIM! NILAMADHAV — THE GOD WHO IS BLUE IN COLOUR! HE SHALL BE THE ONE TO GRACE MY TEMPLE.
BUT... WHERE IS NILACHALA HILL? WHERE DO I LOOK FOR IT?
THE VERY NEXT DAY HE SPOKE TO HIS TRUSTED MEN ABOUT THE DREAM.
FIND THE HILL AND THE IMAGE AND REPORT TO ME. I SHALL THEN GO AND BRING NILAMADHAV TO UTKAL MYSELF.
WE SHALL LEAVE IMMEDIATELY, MY LORD.

THE OFFICERS SET OUT IN DIFFERENT DIRECTIONS IN SEARCH OF NILACHALA.
AMONG THEM WAS A YOUNG MAN NAMED VIDYAPATI.
SOMETHING TELLS ME THAT I SHOULD RIDE INTO THE JUNGLES... THAT I AM BOUND TO FIND THE HILL THERE.
BUT WHEN HE REACHED THE JUNGLES —
NILACHALA, DID YOU SAY ? HMM... NO. NO, NEVER HEARD OF IT.
SORRY, STRANGER, I'VE LIVED HERE A LONG TIME BUT NILACHALA MEANS NOTHING TO ME. I THINK YOU'VE COME TO THE WRONG PLACE.
THESE REPLIES WERE VERY DISCOURAGING. VIDYAPATI, HOWEVER, DID NOT GIVE UP HOPE. CAREFULLY AND PAINSTAKINGLY, HE COMBED THE JUNGLES...
...BUT HE COULD NOT LOCATE NILACHALA.

DAYS WENT BY. HE HAD FINISHED ALL THE FOOD AND WATER HE HAD BROUGHT WITH HIM.
I SHOULD GO TO THE NEAREST VILLAGE FOR SOME FOOD AND WATER.
BUT WHEN HE MOUNTED HIS HORSE...
...INSTEAD OF RIDING OUT OF THE JUNGLE HE RODE DEEPER AND DEEPER INTO IT.
NILACHALA, WHEREVER YOU ARE, I'LL FIND YOU...
THE DEEPER HE WENT THE DENSER THE JUNGLE BECAME.
FINALLY HE HAD TO DISMOUNT, LEAVE HIS HORSE BEHIND AND HACK HIS WAY THROUGH.

AT LAST, AFTER DAYS, HE MANAGED TO FIND HIS WAY OUT OF THE JUNGLE.
FAINT WITH HUNGER AND THIRST, HE STAGGERED UP TO A TREE...
...AND LOWERED HIMSELF TO THE GROUND. SUDDENLY—
WHAT'S ...THAT SOUND ? THE TINKLING OF BELLS...SOME-ON SINGING R IS IT A DREAM ?
IT WAS NOT A DREAM. IT WAS A REAL COWHERD COMING THAT WAY WITH HIS COWS.
LA, LA, LA, LA... AAA...
WHEN THE BOY SAW VIDYAPATI HE RAN UP TO HIM.
YOU POOR MAN ! HERE! DRINK THIS.
THE MILK WAS SWEET AND WARM AND REVIVED VIDYAPATI INSTANTLY!
YOU LOOK LIKE A MAN FROM THE CITY. WHAT ARE YOU DOING HERE?
I AM LOOKING FOR A HILL NAMED NILACHALA, CHILD. DO YOU KNOW WHERE IT IS?

I KNOW WHERE IT IS, BUT I WON'T TELL YOU. LOOK FOR IT YOURSELF. SEARCH WITH FAITH AND SINCERITY AND I'M SURE YOU'LL FIND IT!
AND THE LITTLE COWHERD VANISHED. VIDYAPATI FELL TO THINKING.
COULD... COULD THAT BOY HAVE BEEN LORD NILA-MADHAV HIMSELF COME TO GIVE ME HOPE? I'M CERTAIN NOW THAT NILACHALA IS SOMEWHERE NEAR BY.
AS VIDYAPATI CONTINUED HIS SEARCH HE CAME TO A BEAUTIFUL STREAM.
I'VE BEEN WANDERING ALONE FOR SOME DAYS NOW. WHEN WILL I BE IN THE COMPANY OF PEOPLE AGAIN AND HEAR HUMAN VOICES?
JUST THEN —
HA, HA, HA! DON'T SPLASH! YOU'LL SOAK ME! HA, HA, HA!
OH! MY PITCHER! MY PITCHER'S FLOATING AWAY!
AND A GIRL APPEARED ROUND THE BEND OF THE STREAM.
I'VE GOT YOU, YOU NAUGHTY PITCHER!

OH! A STRANGER! WHAT'S HE DOING HERE?
DO NOT BE AFRAID, BEAUTIFUL MAIDEN. I AM VIDYAPATI FROM UTKAL.
I LOST MY WAY IN THE JUNGLE.
OH! I SEE. I AM LALITA, DAUGHTER OF THE SAVARA CHIEFTAIN, VISHVAVASU.
COME WITH ME, I'LL TAKE YOU TO MY FATHER.
WHEN THEY REACHED THE TRIBAL VILLAGE—
FATHER, THIS IS A STRANGER FROM FAR AWAY UTKAL. HE LOST HIS WAY IN THE JUNGLES.
WELCOME TO OUR VILLAGE, SIR. STAY WITH US AWHILE AS OUR GUEST.

VIDYAPATI, AFTER HIS DAYS OF LONELY WANDERING, WAS ONLY TOO GLAD TO STAY WITH THE SAVARAS.
WHAT HOSPITABLE PEOPLE THEY ARE!
SHOULD I TELL THEM ABOUT MY SEARCH FOR NILAMADHAV? NOT YET, PERHAPS.
SOON VIDYAPATI'S GROWING LOVE FOR THE SAVARAS BEGAN TO CENTRE UPON THEIR CHIEF'S DAUGHTER — YOUNG LALITA.
HOW KIND AND GOOD LALITA IS! AND LOVELIER THAN THE LOVELIEST OF FLOWERS!
THE STRANGER AND LALITA LOOK AT EACH OTHER WITH EYES OF LOVE. HMM...
WHEN VIDYAPATI AND LALITA EXPRESSED THEIR WISH TO BE MARRIED, VISHVAVASU HEARTILY GAVE HIS CONSENT AND HIS BLESSINGS. AND SOON —
THE MARRIED COUPLE SPENT MANY HAPPY HOURS TOGETHER.

IT WAS AROUND THAT TIME THAT VIDYAPATI NOTICED SOMETHING WHICH INTRIGUED HIM.
THERE HE GOES AGAIN!
LALITA, I SEE YOUR FATHER GOING OUT AT DAWN EVERY DAY AND RETURNING ONLY AT DUSK. WHERE DOES HE GO?
SSSH! DON'T SPEAK SO LOUDLY. IT'S A CLOSELY-GUARDED SECRET.
TO BE KEPT EVEN FROM YOUR HUSBAND?
NO... NO... WHY SHOULD I HIDE IT FROM YOU?
MY FATHER GOES DEEP INTO THE JUNGLE TO A CAVE ON A HILL.
A CAVE ON A HILL, DID YOU SAY?
YES, THE CAVE OF THE GREAT LORD NILAMADHAV, ON NILACHALA HILL.
NILACHALA! NILAMADHAV!

DEAR ONE, PLEASE ASK YOUR FATHER TO TAKE ME TO THE CAVE OF NILAMADHAV.
OH! I DON'T THINK HE WILL AGREE. BUT I'LL ASK HIM.
AS LALITA HAD EXPECTED, VISHVAVASU WAS NOT VERY HAPPY WHEN SHE MADE THE REQUEST TO HIM.
LALITA, HOW COULD YOU REVEAL MY PRECIOUS SECRET TO HIM!
IS HE NOT ONE OF US NOW? FATHER, PLEASE LET HIM SEE THE LORD. JUST ONCE. PLEASE, FATHER.
LALITA'S PLEADINGS FINALLY WORKED.
ALL RIGHT, I WILL TAKE YOU, VIDYAPATI. BUT BLINDFOLDED.
BLINDFOLDED? BUT I MUST KNOW THE WAY TO NILACHALA. YES...I THINK I KNOW WHAT TO DO...
THAT NIGHT, VIDYAPATI STOLE INTO THE KITCHEN, TOOK A HANDFUL OF SOMETHING FROM A JAR...
...AND QUIETLY WENT BACK TO BED.
THE NEXT DAY VIDYAPATI WAS READY EARLY. AND SOON—
I AM SORRY I HAVE TO BLINDFOLD YOU, MY SON. BUT NILAMADHAV IS MY GOD AND I GUARD HIM LIKE A TREASURE.
I HOPE THE MUSTARD SEEDS I TOOK FROM THE KITCHEN WILL DO THEIR WORK!

AND THE WALK TO THE CAVE BEGAN.
FORGIVE ME, MY FATHER-IN-LAW, BUT WHAT I AM DOING...
...I AM DOING FOR MY KING.
THE WALK SEEMED ENDLESS TO VIDYAPATI. THEN HE FELT THE LEVEL LAND GIVE WAY TO A RISING SLOPE.
WE ARE BEGINNING TO CLIMB. THIS MUST BE NILACHALA HILL.
VIDYAPATI'S HEART BEGAN TO THUMP WITH EXCITEMENT.
WHEN THEY REACHED THE CAVE, VISHVAVASU REMOVED THE BANDAGE. BUT ONLY FOR A FEW MOMENTS.
LOOK ON HIM, MY SON.
BEAUTIFUL! HE IS BEAUTIFUL...
THEN THE BANDAGE WAS BACK ON VIDYAPATI'S EYES.
LET ME GO! LET ME GO! I MUST HAVE ANOTHER GLIMPSE! I MUST...
GET A HOLD ON YOURSELF, VIDYAPATI, THIS IS MY CAVE AND MY GOD. BE THANKFUL I SHARED AT LEAST A GLIMPSE OF HIM WITH YOU. NOW, LET'S GO BACK.
AND VISHVAVASU LED VIDYAPATI BACK HOME.

BUT VIDYAPATI DID NOT HAVE TO WAIT LONG TO SEE THE IMAGE AGAIN FOR THE RAINS SOON SET IN.
POUR RAIN, POUR HARD. WATER MY MUSTARD SEEDS SO THEY WILL SPROUT AND FLOWER!
A FEW DAYS LATER —
MY MUSTARD SEEDLINGS HAVE GROWN BEAUTIFULLY! THE PATH OF YELLOW FLOWERS WILL LEAD ME STRAIGHT TO THE LORD.
FOLLOWING THE TRAIL OF MUSTARD PLANTS, VIDYAPATI BROKE INTO A RUN...
...AND REACHED THE CAVE.
JUST AS THE KING SAID — IT IS THE MOST BEAUTIFUL IMAGE EVER SEEN!

VIDYAPATI HAD FOUND NILAMADHAV FOR HIS KING ! REJOICING, HE RETURNED TO THE VILLAGE AND TOOK LEAVE OF THE SAVARA CHIEF.
SIR, I MUST NOW RETURN TO MY OWN KINGDOM. PLEASE GIVE LALITA AND ME YOUR BLESSINGS.
I WILL MISS YOU.
WHEN THEY REACHED UTKAL, VIDYAPATI WENT STRAIGHT TO THE PALACE.
MY LORD, I HAVE FOUND NILACHALA AND NILAMADHAV.
LEAD ME TO NILA-CHALA AT ONCE, DEAR VIDYAPATI!
SOON, WITH VIDYAPATI LEADING THE WAY, INDRADYUMNA AND HIS QUEEN, GUNDICHA DEVI, SET OUT FOR NILACHALA.
ON THE WAY —
MY QUEEN, CAN YOU BELIEVE IT? I, INDRADYUMNA, WILL BE THE ONE WHO DIS-COVERED NILAMADHAV FOR THE OUTSIDE WORLD! I WILL TAKE HIM AWAY FROM THAT SELFISH VISHVAVASU AND MAKE HIM MINE ALONE!
MY LORD — DON'T SPEAK SO! DON'T THINK SO! GOD BELONGS TO EVERYONE.
VIDYAPATI HAS TOLD US HOW POSSESSIVE THE SAVARA CHIEFTAIN IS TOWARDS NILAMADHAV. NOW YOU TOO WANT TO MAKE NILAMADHAV YOURS ALONE. BEWARE, MY LORD, OF SUCH THOUGHTS.

BUT THE DAMAGE WAS DONE. ALL GUNDICHA'S WISE WORDS COULD NOT PREVENT THE EFFECT OF INDRADYUMNA'S UNWORTHY THOUGHTS ON NILAMADHAV. THE GENTLE WINDS THAT TILL THEN HAD CARESSED NILACHALA...
...IN A MATTER OF MINUTES, TURNED INTO A FURIOUS SANDSTORM.
THEN, AS SUDDENLY AS IT HAD BEGUN, THE STORM ABATED. BUT THE HILL, THE CAVE AND EVEN THE MUSTARD PLANTS WITH THE YELLOW FLOWERS HAD VANISHED.
NILAMADHAV HAD HIDDEN HIMSELF FROM THE EYES OF MEN.
LATER, WHEN INDRADYUMNA AND VIDYAPATI ARRIVED THERE —
WHERE IS THE HILL? MY CAVE? MY NILAMADHAV?
MY LORD, I... I CAN'T UNDERSTAND. THE TRAIL OF MUSTARD PLANTS ENDS ABRUPTLY HERE. AND BEYOND THEM NOTHING BUT SAND!

CONTD. ON PAGE 18

Suppandi and his friends are all packed!

LATER AS VIDYAPATI LOOKED HELPLESSLY ON, INDRADYUMNA BROKE DOWN.
O VIDYAPATI! MY YEARNING FOR NILAMADHAV IS DRIVING ME MAD. WILL THE LORD NOT SHOW ME A WAY TO REACH HIM?
INDRADYUMNA WEPT LIKE A CHILD...
...TILL HE FELL ASLEEP. AND THEN HE HAD ANOTHER MARVELLOUS DREAM.
O KING, YOUR TEARS HAVE MOVED ME. BUT I CANNOT APPEAR AGAIN AS NILAMADHAV, IN WHICH FORM I AM LOST TO THE WORLD FOR EVER. INSTEAD, I SHALL APPEAR IN THE FORM OF A DAARU* FLOATING ON THE SEA.
TURN BACK AND GO TO THE SEASHORE. I SHALL COME...
AND INDRADYUMNA AWOKE, REFRESHED AND OVERJOYED.
THE NEXT MORNING INDRADYUMNA AND HIS MEN RODE SWIFTLY TO THE SEASHORE.
THEY STOOD ON THE BEACH, SCANNING THE SEA IN ALL DIRECTIONS.

* THE CONCH, WHEEL, MACE AND LOTUS, THE FOUR SYMBOLS OF VISHNU

COME ON! NOW PULL!
THE ELEPHANT TRIED HARD TO MOVE FORWARD BUT ONLY SANK TO ITS KNEES WITH THE EFFORT.
MY LORD, THE DAARU HASN'T MOVED AN INCH. I THINK WE'LL NEED MORE THAN ONE ELEPHANT TO PULL IT ASHORE.
ALL RIGHT. HARNESS EVERY MAN AND ANIMAL TO THE DAARU.
YES, MY LORD.
AS SOON AS THAT WAS DONE —
COME ON, NOW USE ALL YOUR STRENGTH AND PULL.

BUT —
WHY HAS THE LORD PUT THIS SECOND OBSTACLE IN MY PATH ?
IT'S IMPOSSIBLE, MY LORD. THE DAARU JUST WON'T MOVE.
AT A COMPLETE LOSS, INDRADYUMNA CLOSED HIS EYES AND BEGAN TO PRAY TO VISHNU. THEN HE HEARD A VOICE.
O INDRADYUMNA, YOU STILL KEEP MY BELOVED DEVOTEE VISHVAVASU IN CHAINS ! FREE HIM AT ONCE ! ONLY IF THE TWO OF YOU TOGETHER LIFT ME UP SHALL I CONSENT TO BE MOVED.
REALISATION DAWNED ON INDRADYUMNA. HE RUSHED TO THE TENT WHERE VISHVAVASU WAS HELD PRISONER AND EMBRACED HIM.
VISHVAVASU, MY DEAR FRIEND, CAN YOU EVER FORGIVE ME ? WE BOTH LOVE THE SAME LORD AND YET, I WAS MEAN AND SMALL ENOUGH TO DENY HIM TO YOU.
AND INDRADYUMNA TOLD VISHVAVASU ABOUT ALL THAT HAD HAPPENED. THE TWO RIVAL DEVOTEES NOW BROUGHT TOGETHER IN LOVE, WENT UP TO THE DAARU.
COME, LET US LIFT HIM UP TOGETHER.
AND LO !

ARE MY EYES PLAYING TRICKS ON ME?
THE LOG THAT SEVERAL ELEPHANTS AND HORSES COULD NOT PULL, TWO MEN HAVE LIFTED WITH EASE!
THE DAARU WAS BROUGHT OUT OF THE SEA AND INDRADYUMNA, WITH VISHVAVASU'S CONSENT, BEGAN TO MAKE PREPARATIONS TO ENSHRINE IT IN A TEMPLE.
MY LORD, INSTEAD OF ENSHRINING THE DAARU AS IT IS, WHY DON'T WE CARVE IT INTO AN IMAGE OF THE NILA-MADHAV THAT WE LOST?
A WONDERFUL IDEA! I SHALL DESCRIBE THE BEAUTY OF NILAMADHAV TO SKILLED CRAFTSMEN. THEY MAY BE ABLE TO MAKE A REPLICA.
BUT THOUGH MANY EXPERT CRAFTSMEN TRIED TO CARVE THE DAARU, NOT ONE OF THEM WAS SUCCESSFUL.
MY LORD, OUR FINEST AXE-BLADES BREAK THE MOMENT THEY STRIKE THE DAARU!
WE HAVE NOT BEEN ABLE EVEN TO MAKE A NOTCH IN IT.
INDRADYUMNA WAS BAFFLED BY THIS NEW OBSTACLE.
IF THE BEST CRAFTSMEN ON EARTH CANNOT CARVE THE DAARU, WHO CAN?
I CAN, O KING.

AND AN OLD MAN WALKED IN.
I THINK HE IS THE DIVINE ARCHITECT VISHVAKARMA, COME TO EARTH IN DISGUISE.
SIR, IT IS THE IMAGE OF NILAMADHAV WE WANT—BLUE-GREEN IN COLOUR, STUDDED WITH GEMS AND...
WAIT! I AM WILLING TO CARVE THE DAARU, BUT... I WILL SCULPT IT AS I LIKE.
BESIDES, I MUST BE LEFT UNDISTURBED FOR FIFTEEN DAYS IN A SEALED ROOM. ON NO ACCOUNT SHOULD YOU BREAK OPEN THE DOOR. DO YOU AGREE TO THESE TERMS?
I AGREE, NOBLE SIR. PLEASE BEGIN YOUR WORK.
SO THE DAARU WAS TAKEN TO A GREAT HALL AND PLACED ON A MAHAVEDI* AND THE OLD MAN SEALED HIMSELF IN. WHEN TEN DAYS HAD GONE BY GUNDICHA, WHO WAS BY NATURE A PATIENT WOMAN, SUDDENLY BECAME RESTLESS.
MY LORD, WHY IS THERE NO SOUND FROM WITHIN? COULD SOMETHING HAVE HAPPENED TO THE OLD MAN? SHOULDN'T WE OPEN THE DOOR AND SEE?
NO, GUNDICHA, DON'T YOU REMEMBER WHAT HE TOLD US?

* great altar

I DO! I DO! BUT IF HE DIES OF STARVATION OR THIRST WILL WE EVER BE ABLE TO FORGIVE OURSELVES?
OPEN THE DOOR, I BEG YOU. PLEASE OPEN IT!
ALL RIGHT, I'LL OPEN IT.
WHEN INDRADYUMNA HAD THE SEALED DOOR BROKEN OPEN —
THE OLD MAN HAS VANISHED!
OH, NO! WHAT HAVE I DONE!
OH, GUNDICHA, YOU INSISTED ON MY INTERRUPTING THE OLD MAN'S WORK! NOW WE ARE LEFT WITH THREE INCOMPLETE IMAGES.
FORGIVE ME, MY LORD.
JUST THEN, THEY HAD A VISITOR. IT WAS SAGE NARADA HIMSELF!
O INDRADYUMNA, I COME FROM VAIKUNTHA. I'VE BEEN SENT TO TELL YOU THAT YOU SHOULD NOT BE DISAPPOINTED WITH THESE IMAGES. IT IS LORD VISHNU'S WILL THAT THE DAARU SHOULD BE CARVED THUS.
THEN, NOBLE SAGE, I SHALL START WORK ON THE TEMPLE TO ENSHRINE THESE WOODEN IMAGES.

AS THE TEMPLE ON THE SEASHORE WAS BEING BUILT, NEAR BY IN A HUGE ENCLOSURE, HUNDREDS OF COWS WERE HERDED TOGETHER TO BE GIVEN AWAY TO THE POOR.

WHEN THE BUILDING OF THE TEMPLE WAS ABOUT TO BE COMPLETED AND THE COWS HAD BEEN GIVEN AWAY, A HUGE CRATER, LEFT BY THE IMPACT OF THEIR HOOVES, WAS FOUND IN THE ENCLOSURE.

UNDERGROUND STREAMS ROSE TO THE SURFACE AND FED IT WITH CLEAR, SWEET WATER, CREATING A POND.
THIS TANK HAS BECOME A FINE HOME FOR WATER-BIRDS, FISH AND TORTOISES.
LET IT BE KNOWN AS THE INDRA-DYUMNA TANK.

WHEN THE TEMPLE WAS COMPLETED —
MAGNIFICENT! ONLY LORD BRAHMA IS WORTHY OF CONSECRATING IT. LET US BOTH GO AND INVITE HIM TO EARTH.
GUNDICHA WILL BE PLEASED TO HEAR OF THIS.

BUT GUNDICHA WAS FAR FROM PLEASED.
MY LORD, YOU SAY SAGE NARADA IS TAKING YOU TO BRAHMALOKA. I AM AFRAID... I FEEL I SHALL NEVER SEE YOU AGAIN.
HOW TIMID YOU ARE MY DEAR GUNDICHA! I SHALL BE BACK BEFORE YOU KNOW IT!

INDRADYUMNA AND NARADA SOON REACHED BRAHMALOKA.
BUT LORD BRAHMA WAS DEEP IN MEDITATION, SO THEY HAD TO WAIT. HOURS PASSED BY.
WE HAVE BEEN HERE A WHOLE DAY! HOW MUCH LONGER WILL WE HAVE TO WAIT?
JUST THEN, BRAHMA OPENED HIS EYES.
MY LORD, KING INDRADYUMNA HAS BUILT A GLORIOUS TEMPLE TO LORD VISHNU. WOULD YOU COME TO EARTH AND CONSECRATE IT?
I WILL COME. YOU MAY GO AND MAKE THE PREPARATIONS.
INDRADYUMNA AND NARADA HAD SPENT ONLY ONE DAY IN BRAHMALOKA. BUT WHAT THEY FAILED TO REALISE WAS THAT ONE DAY OF BRAHMA IS EQUAL TO THOUSANDS OF YEARS ON EARTH! TO THEM IT MIGHT HAVE SEEMED THAT ONLY A DAY HAD GONE BY...
...BUT ON EARTH, MANY, MANY SUMMERS HAD COME AND GONE. A THOUSAND KINGS AND DYNASTIES HAD RISEN AND FALLEN! AND EVEN AS INDRADYUMNA WAS RETURNING TO EARTH, A DIFFERENT KING, THOUSANDS OF YEARS AFTER HIS TIME, WAS NOW RULING OVER UTKAL.

THIS KING WAS GALA MADHAV. ONE DAY AS HE WAS RIDING ALONG THE SANDS OF A DESERT—
HISTORIANS SAY THAT UNDER THESE SANDS AN ANCIENT CIVILISATION ONCE FLOURISHED. I WONDER...
OH...!
MY HORSE IS DOWN TOO! WHAT COULD HAVE TRIPPED HIM ON THESE SMOOTH SANDS?
GALA MADHAV BEGAN TO SEARCH THE GROUND NEAR HIS HORSE. THEN HE SAW AN OBJECT JUTTING OUT OF THE SAND.
A PIECE OF CARVING? HOW BEAUTIFUL IT IS!
WITH MOUNTING EXCITEMENT GALA MADHAV BEGAN TO PUSH AWAY THE SAND FROM AROUND THE PIECE OF CARVING AND SOON—
THE SUMMIT OF A TEMPLE DOME! I'VE MADE A GREAT DISCOVERY!

HE IMMEDIATELY ORDERED AN EXCAVATION. THE SANDY SHROUD THAT COVERED THE TEMPLE WAS REMOVED AND INDRADYUMNA'S TEMPLE, BURIED FOR CENTURIES, WAS REVEALED TO GALA MADHAV'S EYES.
GALA MADHAV TOOK OVER THE TEMPLE AND INSTALLED HIS CHOSEN DEITY IN IT.
WHEN INDRADYUMNA AND NARADA DESCENDED TO EARTH —
O SAGE, SOMETHING SEEMS WRONG. EVERYTHING LOOKS SO... SO DIFFERENT. THIS DOES NOT LOOK LIKE THE TOWN I LEFT YESTERDAY.
NO! OH, NO! WHAT A FOOL I HAVE BEEN!
IT WAS ONLY THEN THAT THE AWFUL TRUTH DAWNED ON NARADA, BUT TOO LATE.
GENTLY HE BROKE IT TO INDRADYUMNA, EXPLAINING THE VAST DIFFERENCE IN TIME BETWEEN BRAHMALOKA AND EARTH. INDRADYUMNA WAS HORRIFIED.
YOU... YOU MEAN THOUSANDS OF YEARS HAVE ALREADY PASSED BY & THEN... THEN ... I AM A STRANGER TO THIS UTKAL — THE ONLY LIVING HUMAN BEING OF MY TIME.
MY GUNDICHA MUST BE DEAD; VIDYAPATI AND MY FRIEND VISHVAVASU MUST BE GONE TOO. HOW UNFORTUNATE I AM!
O KING, DO NOT GRIEVE. HUMAN BEINGS PASS ON, BUT A TEMPLE STANDS THE TEST OF TIME. DEDICATE YOUR LIFE NOW TO YOUR TEMPLE.

INDRADYUMNA AND NARADA BEGAN TO SEARCH FOR THE TEMPLE. THEY SOON FOUND IT.
THERE IT IS! BUT... SOME WORSHIP IS ALREADY GOING ON INSIDE...
COME ON. WE'LL GO IN AND FIND OUT.
STRUGGLING PAST THE GUARDS AT THE DOOR, THEY RUSHED INTO THE SANCTUM AND THERE —
OH, NO! THE TEMPLE I BUILT WITH SO MUCH LOVE HAS BEEN TAKEN OVER BY SOMEBODY ELSE!
SILENCE! HOW DARE YOU INTERRUPT THE ROYAL WORSHIP OF GALA MADHAV, KING OF UTKAL! WHO ARE YOU?
I, INDRADYUMNA, AM THE KING OF UTKAL. AND THIS TEMPLE IS MINE!
OH! SO WE HAVE A MADMAN HERE!
AS INDRADYUMNA STOOD TONGUE-TIED AND CONFUSED, NARADA LED GALA MADHAV OUTSIDE.
LISTEN, GALA MADHAV, THIS MAN IS THE KING WHO ORIGINALLY BUILT THIS TEMPLE. HE REIGNED HERE A LONG, LONG AGO. YOU MUST GIVE BACK HIS TEMPLE TO HIM.
ARE... ARE YOU MAD TOO? A KING FROM LONG AGO? THEN HOW IS HE STILL ALIVE TODAY? WHAT KIND OF STORY ARE YOU TELLING ME?

WHERE IS THE PROOF THAT THIS IS HIS TEMPLE?
PROOF? ALL THE PEOPLE I KNEW ARE DEAD AND GONE. WHAT PROOF CAN I GIVE?

IF YOU ARE WILLING TO BELIEVE AN OLD TORTOISE THEN I WILL GIVE YOU PROOF!
WHAT... WHO IS THAT?

A HUGE TORTOISE ROSE UP FROM THE TANK.
MY NAME IS AKUPAR. I REMEMBER YOU, INDRADYUMNA. I HAVE LIVED FOR CENTURIES IN THIS TANK WHICH WAS ONCE NAMED AFTER YOU. A TORTOISE HAS A LONG MEMORY. YES, IT WAS YOU WHO BUILT THIS TEMPLE.

JUST THEN, LORD BRAHMA APPEARED.
LORD BRAHMA HIMSELF! FORGIVE ME, INDRADYUMNA FOR REFUSING TO BELIEVE YOU.

* INSTALLATION CEREMONY

SUBSCRIBE NOW!

TINKLE MAGAZINE		TINKLE DIGEST		TINKLE COMBO MAGAZINE + DIGEST	
 FREE* ACK DVD worth ₹149 *with 2 year subscription		 FREE ACK DVD worth ₹149		 FREE TIME COMPASS DVD worth ₹598	
1 yr subscription	2 yr subscription	1 yr subscription	2 yr subscription	1 yr subscription	2 yr subscription
Pay only ~~₹480~~ ₹380!	Pay only ~~₹960~~ ₹750!	Pay only ~~₹720~~ ₹580!	Pay only ~~₹1440~~ ₹1080!	Pay only ~~₹1200~~ ₹880!	Pay only ~~₹2400~~ ₹1680!

I would like a subscription for

TINKLE MAGAZINE ☐ 1 yr | ☐ 2 yrs | **TINKLE COMBO** ☐ 1 yr | ☐ 2 yrs | **TINKLE DIGEST** ☐ 1 yr | ☐ 2 yrs

(Please tick the appropriate box)

YOUR DETAILS*

Name: .... Date of Birth: |_|_| / |_|_| / |_|_|_|_|

Address: ....

.... City: .... Pin: |_|_|_|_|_|_| State: ....

School: .... Class: ....

Tel: .... Mobile: + 91 - |_|_|_|_|_|_|_|_|_|_|

Email: .... Signature: ....

PAYMENT OPTIONS

☐ Cheque /DD:

Please enclose Cheque /DD no. |_|_|_|_|_|_| drawn in favour of 'ACK Media Direct Ltd.'

at .... (bank) for the amount .... ,

dated |_|_| / |_|_| / |_|_|_|_| and send it to: IBH Books & Magazines Distributers Pvt. Ltd., Arch No. 30, West Approach, Below Mahalaxmi Bridge, Mahalaxmi (W), Mumbai - 400034.

☐ Pay Cash on Delivery: Pay cash on delivery of the first issue to the postman. (Additional charge of ₹50 applicable)

☐ Pay by money order: Pay by money order in favour of "ACK Media Direct Ltd."

☐ Online subscription: Please visit: www.amarchitrakatha.com

For any queries or further information: Email: customerservice@ack-media.com or Call: 022-40497435 / 36